A Short Collection of Fables

by Fuad A. Kamal

Table of Contents

The Story of the Lions and the Shark

There once was a lioness and her two cubs. The lioness was a great mother and took loving care of her two small cubs, a boy and a girl. She fawned over them on a daily basis, and the two cubs enjoyed playing with each other every day as the mother looked on protectively.

One day, their journey took them in an entirely new direction. That day, their journey happened to lead them to a wide, new expanse of endless water. Having never seen so much water, the cubs stared in awe , as the lioness approached the water with great caution.

Just as they approached the water, a gigantic monstrous creature reared its head above the water. "Bow before your king," it roared. The cubs never having seen such an animal recoiled in terror, whimpering behind their mother. Embarrassed, the boy cub finally managed to compose himself and shout back, "Who are you?"

The creature replied, "I am a shark. the ruler of all that I survey around me." Then to emphasize his point, he pound his mighty tail, unleashing a huge wave that broke around the lions, thoroughly wetting them. He then leaped ten feet into the air and menacingly bared his enormous teeth at the lions, before coming crashing down, causing another gigantic wave that drenched the terrified cubs. Even the fish that had been previously meandering peacefully along the edge of the water all scattered in fear – not wishing to annoy the mighty creature.

Being inexperienced in the ways of the world, the boy cub managed to mumble, "You are not as great as my mom and dad." Meanwhile, his older sister simply wondered what her silly little brother was saying.

On hearing the cub's words, the shark become furious. "Only I am your ruler! Bow before me at once." With that, and with his fury at a maximum, he hurled himself at the male cub to teach him a lesson.

Out of the corner of her eye, the lioness saw the huge creature hurling through the air directly at her son. Without thinking twice about the enormous danger to herself, she leaped into the air to position herself between the shark and her cub. There was a mighty thud as the two powerful creatures collided forcefully into each other, and a mighty desperate battle began...

Then it ended almost as soon as it had started.

To everyone's surprise (including the shark's), his landing on the ground seemed to render him almost helpless. The once mighty animal struggled simply to survive on the ground. While mighty on the water, he was a puny creature on the land. Yet, even in this helpless state the shark incredulous as he was, could not help himself and yelled, "Bow before your king."

Now, even the cubs could see the ridiculousness of the situation and could not help suppressing a giggle or two. Their mother had had enough. With her two cubs in tow, she simply walked away – her head held high.

As they headed back to their base camp, the father lion saw his wife and kids returning from their foray. The lion asked the returning lioness, "So how was your day?" "Nothing eventful, dear," replied the lioness. "Nothing eventful?" the cubs cried incredulously. "Dad, you had to see mom. It was awesome," yelled the cubs.

Moral of the story: If you are a lion/lioness, and your adversary is a shark, engage on land — not in the water. Alternatively, if you are a shark and your opponent is a lion/lioness make sure you engage in the water — not on the land. Know your own (and your challenger's) strengths and weaknesses *before* you challenge him (or her).

The Day that Ignorance Sought to be King

Once upon a time, Truth and Falsehood had an argument. Falsehood said he deserved to rule the village of Wealth because he was more powerful. Truth disagreed. Therefore, they went before Justice to present their case.

Ignorance (an alias that Falsehood also went by) told them, "Give me a day, and I will have the village of Wealth under my grip." Justice agreed. The next day, Ignorance approached the village chief and told him that his rival was plotting to kill him and to take over. The chief rushed to investigate with sword in hand.

However, it was one of those days where nothing moves faster than Ignorance. "Did you know that the village chief is coming to kill you with his sword?" Fear, Ignorance's younger brother and ally, asked the village rival. "You better be ready for him!" continued Fear. The village rival immediately picked up his sword.

Ignorance was left spending the rest of the day chuckling as the two main clans fell upon each other. By the end of the day, Ignorance reigned triumphant. Clearly, the village had fallen to him. He approached Justice and asked him for the village. Truth was quiet and looked tiny before a now towering and gloating Ignorance. Justice was forced to yield the village to Ignorance. Justice and Truth looked at each other in quiet desperation, as Ignorance took command of the village. However, as time passed, the prosperous village became poor; the weeds overran the fields. Ignorance began to lose interest in commanding a declining empire.

At this time, Hope and Youth visited Truth and asked him, "Why have you stood still and not said anything?"

"No one wanted me," replied Truth. "We want you!" replied Hope and Youth. With those three magical words, Truth grew 10 feet taller.

"Let us confront the village chief," said Hope and Youth to Truth. Justice barely managed to suppress a widening smile. Truth grew 20 feet taller.

Ignorance (who was actually quite lazy) took one look at the now formidable, towering figure of Truth and fled. "Who needs the aggravation of this moth-eaten, devastated village anyway?" Ignorance declared as he beat a hasty retreat.

As Truth glowed, the village's weeds were replaced by fruit trees and the stagnant water with flowing streams. Truth reigned, and Justice was pleased with the new king.

Wisdom, Truth's uncle, said, "Ignorance is very powerful, but he can only conquer with darkness. The more powerful he becomes, the more he devours all light around him. Finally, he consumes himself. Only Truth can truly reign over the real soul of Wealth."

"Wealth has found its true king!" Justice declared.

The Man, the Mosquito and the Hut

"Shall I tell you the story of the man and the mosquito?" the storyteller asked.

"Yes," the villagers chimed enthusiastically.

"Well, there was once a large man who awoke bitten by a tiny mosquito. Being rightly aggrieved, he searched for his axe to squash the pesky bugger. 'Ah! There!' the man grunted as he wielded his axe directly at the mosquito. Missed! He heard a loud crunch of wood in the dark.

"He adjusted himself a little better and rubbed his eyes. The mosquito almost seemed to dance its way to the wall on his left. The man felt a slight twang of irritation. He squinted his eyes and swung his axe against the insect. He just missed, but he thought he had clipped part of the mosquito's wing. He swung again—this time a little faster, harder. He felt a thud; the wall beam cracked, but where was that mosquito? He must have gotten it.

"He felt a little uncertain and was still half asleep. However, he was tired, and so he more of less rolled back into his bed. A few moments later, he heard the telltale buzz of his mosquito. He was getting really annoyed.

"He leaped out his bed furiously swinging his axe back and forth. The man marveled at how quickly he smashed his axe against the hut walls. There was no way for the mosquito to escape now. His axe was a whirl of action against the backdrop of his hut. That must have done it. 'The mosquito is certainly no more,' he declared most emphatically after a few minutes of action.

"He barely finished before, out of the corner of his eye, he saw the walls begin to collapse around him. He rushed out of his hut just in time before the roof of his hut fell in."

At this point, the storyteller was interrupted. "All this just for a mosquito? I also heard that story. In fact, it was not a mosquito, but a mosquito and a bat," another villager piped in."

"Both of you are wrong. It was not a mosquito or just a bat. It was a three, big, bloodthirsty vampire bats," a second villager jumped in.

The storyteller stopped and said, "It was a mosquito." The storyteller then continued ...

"As the man slowly began to realize what had just happened, he thought it wise to sit down. As he looked into his large hands, he wondered just how he was going to phrase the events that transpired when his diminutive, yet so articulate wife, returned to their hut later that day. 'Maybe I just should have swatted the mosquito with my hands,' the big man thought ruefully."

Moral of the story: React proportionately to a perceived slight or injury, least by overreacting you find yourself losing a part of who you are.

The Secret Ingredient

One day, a beautiful, but inexperienced, star was about to feed her child Earth. Star carefully read the ingredients for the nourishment she was going to provide Earth. She wanted to give her child everything– as any loving mother would. So she carefully weighed the ingredients she could provide. However, she also had a secret weapon, a crystal ball that would help validate her decisions.

The first recipe she examined only seemed to have fillers, and she doubted it would benefit Earth. Her crystal ball concurred, giving Earth prognosis of "Lost" for a diet laden only with fillers.

So she flipped over to next one. This one seemed promising. It only had one ingredient, but it was the most beautiful and delicate ingredient she had ever seen. It was simply labeled "Compassion." How happy she was! She had found her gift for her child. She barely had time to glance at the crystal ball. To her surprise, as the crystal ball balanced the worst of all the trials her child Earth would face with Star's gift, it sadly flashed one word: "Ineffective."

Star was crestfallen, but she still had pages left in the book. The next recipe also only had one ingredient. This ingredient was the best dressed, most elegant and eloquent ingredient she had ever seen, and its name was "Truth." It exuded such force that she felt confident that she had found her gift. Nonetheless, she decided to check with her crystal ball. As the crystal ball assembled the worst of the trials Earth would face, it shuddered and responded simply with one word: "Insensitive."

Star realized this was going to be more complicated than she had thought, but she still was hopeful. She turned the page. This recipe was a little different. This time, she poured "Compassion" in and watched the crystal ball flash "Ineffective." Next, the directions asked her to add "Truth" to her mixture and to shake. The crystal ball immediately switched away from "Ineffective" and began to hum contentedly as it fluttered through the possibilities. Star was excited; maybe this change in process would open a world of possibilities. Her excitement quickly stopped; the crystal ball had emitted a single word: "Chaos."

Star realized that this was not going to be solved merely by a process change. She would have to dig deeper. She resolutely turned the page to the next and final recipe. It offered a completely new element. Its ingredient was the most perfectly symmetrical shaped piece of ice she had ever seen. Its name was "Justice." Star eagerly glanced at her crystal ball, her hopes high. The crystal ball digested Star's input and began to calculate the possible futures. Suddenly, the crystal ball began to shake, and it shuddered so violently that Star thought it would break. Finally, the ball spit out one word: "Revolt."

Star began to look a little worried. Recipe book or not, her child would have a protecting gift from her mother. Without a thought, Star took "Justice" and "Compassion" and mixed them together. "How could this extraordinary combination fail?" she asked herself.

The crystal ball churned through the possibilities mightily. Finally, it had an answer. The answer left Star in shock. It simply read: "Injustice."

Star confidence in herself was severely shaken as she realized what she had almost done to her child in her ignorance. Timidly, she forced herself to add "Justice" and "Truth." Once again, the crystal ball spun wildly. Star's heart dropped when it responded: "Arrogance."

Star was desperate. She felt like giving up. Was she doing her child more harm than good? Then it struck her. She knew what to do. She did not hesitate. "Truth, Justice, and Compassion" were all mixed together. The crystal ball computed instantly, like it had hit the jackpot: "Balanced ecosystem," it read. Then, the two words faded and were replaced by a glowing white light that gave Star a great deal of peace. She had her gift.

Star quietly added a card to her gift. It did not need many words of explanation:

Recipes
RESULT/INPUTS OUTPUT

Justice	Truth	Compassion	Issue(s)?
No	No	No	Lost
No	No	Yes	Ineffective
No	Yes	No	Insensitive
No	Yes	Yes	Chaos
Yes	No	No	Revolt
Yes	No	Yes	Injustice
Yes	Yes	No	Arrogance

| Yes | Yes | Yes | Balance |

Star looked at her child. Finally, filled with joy, she began to shine. That night, she shone so brightly she was the brightest star in the night sky.

The Boy who Played with Stones

"So you will tell me how to earn a hundred dollars?" the boy asked the old man with a wild-eyed look.

"Even better, I will show you how to earn a *million* dollars," the old man said. The boy simply nodded, slightly in shock. "Just spend some time with me tomorrow and one day every week for the next two years."

"That seems a tad too simple," the boy said somewhat suspiciously.

"Simple is sometimes difficult." the old man answered mysteriously. "In fact, if you can, just give me some of your time for the next two years, and I can get you your equivalent of a billion dollars."

"Is a billion more than a million?" the boy asked. His math skills were still a little shaky.

The old man broke into the biggest smile the boy had ever seen, "Yes, indeed," he replied.

So the boy scampered off with a grin on his face, and he did, indeed, return to the old man for the next few days. Then one day before he was about to leave for his daily trip, he was interrupted. "Before you rush off again today," his best friend said, "why don't you play with me by the creek a little."

So the two kids stopped by the creek. "What a shiny, little stone," the best friend cried.

"Hey, I found one, too", the boy replied. Before they

knew it, it was beginning to get dark. Yet, they had had such a grand time with their shiny stones. The boy missed the old man, but he could always go tomorrow. However, even with that seemingly harmless thought, his memory of the old man faded just a little bit.

That day as the sun set, the old man knew that the boy would not come, but he would wait. As it was, 10 feet below the old man's feet, buried deep, lay a mighty treasure that would unlock for its rightful owner all the treasures of a world. However, the boy never came back, so he waited.

Then another day, just after dawn, another, new boy walked in. Might things be different this time? the old man thought.

Moral of the story: The distraction of "shiny stones" and the dulling pull of procrastination can easily fell one's path to true enduring success.

The Magnificent Flight of the Birds

A great conference of birds had been called. "What is all this commotion?" Grasshopper asked while perched on Owl's shoulder. "They are going to elect our next leader," Owl replied. As the different squads of eagles, falcons, parrots, and other birds gathered to debate, the air began to get tense. No one wanted to let the other group rule. Finally, an elder said, "Why not have this momentous decision be settled by what we birds revel in most, what we hold most dear: flight." As such, the first grand flight was declared. It would be a grueling flight to Hook Mountain and back, and the bird who completed it first would be the next leader.

"Are you going to take part?" Grasshopper asked excitedly.

"Well, owls are not usually known for their speed ..." Owl started to reply.

"So you are just going to give up?" Grasshopper asked despondently.

Just then, Owl accidentally glanced up to see a magnificent eagle chatting with a rather pretty, young owl that he had noticed earlier. The eagle seemed to alternate between preening himself, talking to the attractive owl, and dramatically waving his entry ticket for the race. "Well, if I really wanted to, I am sure I could do the race," the male owl muttered most unexpectedly.

"Really?" Grasshopper perked up.

"I am sure I could win!" he began nonchalantly, but ended with a hint of irritation. That eagle was spending way too much time with the pretty young owl.

Grasshopper looked over to where his friend was glancing. "Hey, guess what, my friend Owl will win the race," he yelled. The young owl looked over her shoulder in surprise and smiled. The grasshopper's friend was the only owl who was going to take part in a competition that seemed to be filled with eagles and falcons.

Owl looked embarrassed as the camp broke out into laughter. "Tact, Grasshopper, tact," Owl whispered violently.

"I thought you said you could win," Grasshopper replied. Just then, the pretty young owl waved. Owl had his entry ticket within the next five minutes.

To say that Owl was nervous was probably an understatement. He had just timidly checked the weather forecast, which looked bad. Two words caught his eye: "Highly unstable." He had barely uttered the word "Storm" when Grasshopper simply looked at him and asked, "You are not going to drop out, are you?"

"No, of course, not," Owl replied nervously. After all, He did have a plan. He mustered up all his courage and lined up at the starting line. As the starting gun went off, he executed his plan.

As wave after wave of birds rose mightily from his right, catching the strong prevailing winds, he banked sharply to the left. He would simply sit out this foolhardy quest, out of sight of everyone, and not embarrass himself. He would do the whole course and reappear at the end to cross the finish line after the crowds had left.

"What are you doing in the middle of nowhere? You are completely out in left field. There is not even the hint of a breeze here," Grasshopper exclaimed. Owl was startled, he had forgotten in his daze that Grasshopper must have climbed on his shoulder.

Owl felt embarrassed. What would he tell grasshopper? Finally, he said, "Well, I have a plan."

"To win the race? Here?" Grasshopper asked incredulously.

Owl didn't really have a race plan, per se. He thought quickly, and then it dawned on him. He did have a plan. He flapped his wings and went further to his left.

"Are you insane?" Grasshopper yelled. "Why are you going continually to the left when all the birds have gone to the right?"

"Grasshopper, truth is that there is only one winner. By that count, I have already lost the race unless I take a chance."

"Huh?" said Grasshopper.

"I did check the weather report, Owl replied. "True, the prevailing winds are normally on the right, and there are no winds here. However, the report did predict unstable weather conditions. Perhaps, we will get lucky, and the winds will change."

"That is a very big if and very unlikely," Grasshopper

quipped.

Owl nodded. "Yes, but remember I have already lost the race. As such, I have nothing to lose and everything to gain, if the winds shift."

Owl began to flap his winds and fly the first leg of the race. Owl had been flying for an hour, and he suddenly felt a slight breeze. "Grasshopper, stop joking, you do not need to blow on me." Grasshopper only laughed in response.

They soon settled into a rhythm. After a time, Owl felt a stronger breeze. He turned around; grasshopper's lungs were not that strong. Grasshopper was gesturing frantically. A huge storm front was developing right behind them. Then, it happened, a once in a hundred-year event. A massive wind current began to develop behind them. Owl and Grasshopper were propelled forward so violently that even if Owl had not wanted to race, he had no choice. He was flying forward upside down at an extraordinary speed.

Before he knew it, they had reached Hook Mountain, just as the sudden storm subsided. They were the first ones to check in. Owl wasted no time and immediately began the return leg back. However, he took the normal route back. "What happened to taking chances?" Grasshopper chirped.

"Before, I had nothing to lose. Now, I have everything to lose and nothing to gain," Owl replied. "As long as I take the same route as the other birds, they will not be able to get a wind advantage over me. "

"What if they change routes?" Grasshopper asked.

"I will also change my route to match theirs. We will both have the same wind," Owl replied.

Then and there, Grasshopper realized his friend had already won the race. The next day, to everyone's amazement, Owl was crowned the king of the birds. It was a grand ceremony, but finally it was over, and Owl and Grasshopper had some time to reflect.

"I wanted you to win, but I wasn't sure you would," said Grasshopper.

"Neither was I," said Owl, "but strategy is sometimes more important than raw ability. Now, excuse me; I need to find someone I saw at the finish line."

"Can I come along?" asked Grasshopper, following his friend.

The Most Magnificent Battle

"So it is decided. The battle to decide all battles will be fought tomorrow," The lions of the sky and earth kingdoms announced to their nations.

"However, this will be decided with honor and courage," said the lion king from the sky kingdom.

"Befitting the magnitude of the occasion, the battle between the sky and earth nations may run for several days," the lion king from the earth kingdom continued.

"The victor's reign will encompass all that lies between the two horizons," they both declared.

On the day of the battle, the sky and earth kings called all their subjects into the field of battle. The sky and earth lion kings arranged for even the lowest of their subjects to be able to display their honor and courage on the field. Their tales of battles would be recounted for all generations.

In the first order of battle, the lowest of the subjects, the mice and the chickens from the sky kingdom and the chickens and mice of the earth kingdom, would valiantly fight. Everyone else would watch and make note of the acts of heroism of the day.

Next in the order of battle, when the chickens and mice had concluded their battles of bravery, the second battle would begin. Equally resplendent in their pageantry, the buffaloes, zebras, dogs, cats, and birds of the sky and earth kingdoms would parade onto the battlefield and descend into each other.

Finally, when the second battle concluded, the third and final leg of the war would conclude. The lions, leopards, tigers, and elephants from both kingdoms would then enact the culmination of battle. The highest forms of battle would be displayed.

The order of battle was read. The trumpet was blown. The mice and chicken bedecked in splendid color filled the girth of the valley and were cheered by roaring crowds. It was several hours before they were ready to start the battle.

Then from nowhere, a terrifying roar resounded in the valley. "Prepare to meet your end mice and chickens," the lions and elephants from the earth kingdom roared. Of course the sky mice and chickens were unable to handle the onslaught of the top warriors of the earth kingdom, and those that were unable to scatter from the battlefield were quickly defeated.

The earth elephants, lions, leopards, and tigers wasted no time. They immediately, without warning, unleashed themselves on the sky zebras, buffaloes, dogs, and cats who were arranged right behind the mice and chickens. The result of the lopsided battle was quick, decisive, and unambiguous. The earth lions roared in victory, barely out of breath.

Finally, the earth lions turned to face the sky lions. But before that, they summoned the earth zebras, buffaloes, cats, dogs, mice, and chickens. Together, they launched their last and most ferocious attack.

Now, while the sky lions might have defeated the

earth lions, they were no match for the entire earth kingdom.

It was not long before the earth lion king assumed the throne of all that he could see. The sky kingdom had been completely crushed.

The jubilant and triumphant earth lion king surveyed the expansive swart that the earth kingdom had laid waste. With satisfaction he noted that his dominions stretched beyond what the eye could behold.

The earth creatures were happy. But it did not last. Slowly, almost imperceptibly the mood began to change. A strange quiet loneliness began to seep into the souls of the earth creatures almost as imperceptibly as a black ant meandering silently and aimlessly on a moonless night.

But its subtle pangs soon became definite. There was a terrible empty hole in the hearts of the earth creatures that no amount of wealth could fill. For what was an earth without a sky? Or a sky without an earth? Had they cut out a vital part of themselves, and were now suffering the consequences?

And no one now realized it better than the earth king. When the realization hit him, he was shaken and released a terrible roar, an anguished cry from the inconsolable dark abyss deep within him.

Humbled and crestfallen, the earth lion king knew what he had to do. With his head low, the earth king began his long, shameful walk towards his other half, the inhabitants of the sky. He would fix his terrible mistake, and happiness would return.

For he now knew a terrible truth emerging form the ashes of the battle and the depths of time: The earth had always been broken... before it had been melded with the sky.

Lesson #1: Honor and courage alone cannot win the day.

Lesson #2: Sometimes when you hurt others, you hurt yourself too.

The Pauper Who Would be King

There was once a pauper who had a magnificent dream. He dreamt that he was a mighty king who ruled over a grand kingdom. Convinced that he had been born to royalty, the pauper decided he would claim his birthright.

At once, he decided he would march into the most expensive clothes store in the town. He entered in a most regal manner, a manner befitting his station in life. His appearance startled the clerks. They were initially uncertain how to deal with him. However, being merchants, they inquired if any clothes had caught his fancy. The pauper smiled and motioned in the general direction of the most elegant clothes in the store. After a considerable amount of time trying on any clothes he felt might be remotely befitting of royalty, he felt his task was accomplished. Gesturing towards an amassed pile of clothes, he told the store clerks that he would take the lot. The store workers quickly moved to gather his selection.

"How might you pay?" asked the head store clerk.

"What a silly question," replied the pauper. "You should be pleased that someone of my station is wearing your clothes. Why would I pay you? Hand me my packages."

After a few minutes, it soon became apparent what was happening. The store workers unceremoniously dumped the pauper on the street.

"What a bunch of losers. They will regret this. This no way to treat a king," muttered the pauper as he slowly picked himself up. Naturally being indignant, he grumbled for a considerable time. After a while, he began to feel hungry, and his face broke into a big smile.

The reason for his pleasure was simple: he had decided to dine at the finest restaurant in town —the only dining establishment worthy of a king. As he strutted into the restaurant, his eyes immediately fell on the finest seats in the establishment. Without any hesitation, he placed himself squarely into a commanding position.

Firmly established, he glanced around and beckoned towards the dining server he felt most closely resembled a king's attendant. "Please, present me with your finest dishes at once," he demanded. Although caught by surprise, the waiter rapidly regained his composure and produced an elegant menu. "I cannot decide. Kindly bring a sampling of each of your finest selections," intoned the pauper. Being the town's fanciest eating establishment they quickly complied.

With the staff catering to his every fancy, the pauper settled contentedly into his grand five-course meal. As he began to wipe off the last bit of his plate, he began to feel a little sleepy. He decided to get up in preparation for his departure. The waiters did not know how to react. The head waiter approached and asked uncertainly, "Would you like to settle the bill here or at the counter?"

This drew a hurt rebuke. "This is a most ungracious way to treat a king. It is you that should be honored by my presence. Yet, you have the effrontery to ask for cash."

The waiter apologized, "Unfortunately, this is the ways things work in our town. People pay for their meals."

At this moment the pauper decided to storm out of the restaurant indignantly. People quickly realized what had happened. King or not, the restaurant staff had had enough and decided to dump him on the street. The pauper could not believe the shabby treatment he was receiving. Raising his fist in the air, he decried the lack of civility to which he had been subjected. Consumed by rightful indignation, he proceeded to tell the street, the lamp posts, the stairs, and anything else in the vicinity how this was not the right way to treat a king. After a while, he noticed a rush of people onto the street. Apparently, it was quitting time, and the local establishments were closing. People from a nearby school flowed onto the street in front of him.

A little girl saw a poor, disheveled man lying in a dump on the side of the street, as the people flowed through the street. Being a little concerned, she asked if he was okay. It took no time for the pauper to blurt out his story.

"Why don't you attend the school like I do?" she asked naively.

"Did you not pay any attention, little girl. Perhaps I did not tell you how rudely I was treated," said the pauper getting a little flustered.

"I feel sorry for how you were treated," the little girl replied. "I do not really know how a king should be treated, but my mother says if I work really hard at my studies that it will help me later in life." The pauper rolled his eyes. Why was he even talking to this little girl? Suddenly the girl grew excited as she remembered something, "I think big people also go to the school." Fortunately, he was rescued as the little girl realized she was late.

It was preposterous — imagine that, a young child telling him, a king, what to do. As if he did not know what to do! Who had the time or patience for what the girl suggested.

As he moved on, he smiled broadly. The king had a wonderful day planned for himself.

Moral of the story: There is no substitute for hard work in order to build a person.